14   W9-AJT-817

SEVEN-YEAR-OLD KATIE longs for her soldier father to come home from the war. Her family is just too small now, and she and Mama are lonely in their New York City apartment. But over the months and years of World War II, Katie's idea of what a family is will change....

First her mother's best friend, Louise, comes to live with them. Pregnant Louise misses her own husband who is fighting in the war, and Mama urges her to stay till after the baby is born. It is Katie who bravely takes Louise to the hospital during a surprise blizzard, and baby Rosie becomes like a little sister to her.

Katie is nine when a uniformed messenger delivers the worst possible news. Rosie's love helps; so do the kind words of their elderly neighbor, Mrs. Leitstein. And when the war is finally over, and Mama proposes a brand-new start, Katie must learn to believe in Mrs. Leitstein's wise advice: "Love is risky, but it's worth it."

Touching, humorous, and memorable, *Love You, Soldier* illuminates themes of love and loss with the warmth and depth for which Amy Hest is well known.

Love You, Soldier

by AMY HEST

Four Winds Press   New York
Maxwell Macmillan Canada   Toronto
Maxwell Macmillan International
New York   Oxford   Singapore   Sydney

For my parents, with love,
and for Laura Seacord

Four Winds Press
Macmillan Publishing Company
866 Third Avenue
New York, NY 10022

Maxwell Macmillan Canada, Inc.
1200 Eglinton Avenue East
Suite 200
Don Mills, Ontario M3C 3N1
Macmillan Publishing Company is part of the Maxwell Communication
Group of Companies.
First edition

Printed and bound in the United States of America

10 9 8 7 6 5 4 3 2 1

The text of this book is set in 13 point Electra.
Book design by Christy Hale

Library of Congress Cataloging-in-Publication Data
Hest, Amy.
Love you, soldier / by Amy Hest.
    p.   cm.
Summary: Katie, a Jewish girl living in New York City during World
War II, sees many dynamic changes in her world as she ages from
seven to ten waiting for her father to return from the war.
ISBN 0-02-743635-7
[1. World War, 1939–1945—United States—Fiction.   2. Jews—
Fiction.   3. New York (N.Y.)—Fiction.]   I. Title.
PZ7.H4375Lo   1991
[Fic]—dc20   90-25161

ONE

THE WAR CAME and my father left in a uniform. It was olive green.

The night before, he filled his bag with army things and things from home. A leather notebook and funny socks (I knit them myself), and the sweater that matched (my mother was the one who really knew about knitting). He packed a fountain pen with bottled ink, and a photo in a frame—my mother when she was young, with waves of red-brown hair and jodhpur pants that made her look like a fancy riding lady.

I made him a picture. I worked and worked and

j 42749

it was eight, then nine, and they called, "Bedtime, Katie!" but I begged for more time. Then it was ten, or later, maybe. I was yawning away! But I kept on, until every line was right and every space that needed color was filled in with splendid dabs of it.

And I fell asleep, resting my cheek on the dining room table.

I gave him the picture in the morning. He put down his teacup—it clinked on the saucer—and I told him all about it and he listened, really listened, patting my streaky-blond hair as I talked. The air between us swelled with his spicy after-shave.

"That's me, there, holding your hand and we are having a picnic," I explained. "Just you and me. Mama, too. It is summer and there's this mosquito buzzing all around my knee and sometimes my elbow, and you are saying 'Hey, beat it, man, that knee belongs to me!' Well, off he flies, mad mosquito-man, and we go back to eating. We are eating bread and cheese, and these tiny little chocolates from Murray's. They have sticky caramel centers."

My father wrapped that picture like he was wrapping diamonds. He slipped it in his duffel and zipped the fat brown zipper.

It was time to go to the station.

My mother was all dressed up in her Friday night suit. The synagogue suit. Navy blue with a double row of buttons. Those buttons were pearly white, bigger than quarters. My dress had pleats, and smocking near the collar. And my new party shoes—shiny like mirrors—tapped and clicked on the winding marble stairs.

It was early—morning steam sizzled in rattly old pipes—but the neighbors came out on each landing. They came in housedresses and scuffy bedroom slippers.

There were Mrs. Moskowitz and Mrs. Cook and four little Cooks, who saluted my father. (He saluted back and gave them each a nickel.)

And old Mrs. Leitstein skimmed my father's forehead with pale, quivery lips. She handed him a smallish, flattish box. "Cookies"—she winked— "baked before sunup." (You always knew when Mrs. Leitstein was doing her baking—the whole building was washed with the wondrous smell of it. Later, a plate of cookies would be left on a bench outside her apartment, with a note in her fine print: "Ooops . . . baked too many . . . help yourselves!")

"You go over there and you *win* that war!" Mrs. Leitstein waved a finger in the air and spoke sternly to my father. "Hurry back, soldier." Then, in a whisper, "You come back to us safe and sound . . . you hear?"

My father kissed her crinkly hand the way he'd kiss a queen's hand. "I hear you, Mrs. Leitstein. I hear you loud and clear."

"Good-bye!" called the neighbors. "Good-bye, good-bye!"

" . . . if you find my cousin Johnny over there, you tell him hi from Wanda Bea. . . ."

" . . . maybe you'll see Sid. . . . You must remember my Sid. . . . I'm keeping his comfy chair right by the window. . . . Tell him it's all set up the way he likes it so he can read his papers while I'm fixing chops for his supper. . . ."

"Good-bye!" called the neighbors. "Good-bye, good-bye!"

It was the kind of March day that was more winter than spring. The wind blew off the Hudson River in mighty gusts. Giant clouds—mounds and mounds of them—danced across the sky, and I danced down the street, tapping my heels and twirling.

We took a taxi to the station. This was a grand treat, a taxi to the station. I grabbed the jump seat, of course. It was just a bump of a seat, really, with rusted bouncy springs that squeaked and made me giggle. The driver was a lady. She talked and talked. About the war and far-off places I did not like the sound of.

My parents held hands and never said a single thing all the way from 109th Street to 33rd.

That's a lot of blocks not to talk.

Pennsylvania Station was too big. Too big and too crowded. Everywhere, olive green uniforms like my father's. Soldiers and soldiers and women in colors, hauling babies and flower bouquets and waving white hankies.

"Coming through! Coming through!" Tired-looking redcaps crouched over carts that were loaded up high with luggage. They inched across the jam-packed concourse, and so did we.

There were hollow voices on distant speakers: " . . . now boarding track number two. . . ."

The General Waiting Room was a thousand times bigger than any room I'd ever seen anywhere. There were high, wide arches overhead and a huge clock suspended from the ceiling. But the people! Throngs of them . . . crisscrossing . . . zigzag-ging . . . stepping lively and on the double.

I was pushed and pulled and I was scared. I was

shoved and shuffled. My head felt all dizzy and my stomach felt all scrambled, and I think I cried out "Mama!", stuffing my hand in her blue suit pocket.

" . . . now boarding, track number four. . . ."

My mother gasped.

My father kissed her so hard I couldn't see their faces, and I wished they would stop.

They did stop, finally, when a man selling flowers tapped my father on the shoulder.

My father turned and smiled. And he bought two red roses.

One for my mother.

The other one for me.

He hugged me so hard I thought all the air would be squeezed right out of me. It wasn't, though, and I hugged him back. My hat fell off and he swooped it up, popping it on top of *his* hat—just for a moment—and we laughed.

"Love you, soldier." My mother said that as he stepped on the train.

It sounded nice—*Love you, soldier*—like something that needed a picture.

Up and down that long, long platform there was waving. And calling. Waving. And calling names until my ears were stuffed.

The train whistled and all of me shivered.

The train whistled and then it hissed and lurched and it was moving, and so were all of us left on the platform, waving and calling . . . faster . . . faster . . . then it was gone.

Gone.

Just like that.

A faint whistle wailed in some faraway tunnel, and all of me shivered.

Later, my mother and I wandered toward Fifth Avenue. Just the two of us, and we didn't talk much. She held my hand and never let go, and her gloves were softest leather. They were navy and they closed at the wrist with a button. We walked and walked. My legs were cold, my toes were squished. Party shoes are not walking shoes, I was thinking. I didn't say it, though.

"Empire State Building," I pointed out.

"Mmm-hmm."

"Tallest building in New York, Mama."

"Tallest building in the world, Katie."

And we rode two elevators to the observation deck, high above the city. It was windy! I searched and searched for a train taking soldiers. Maybe *my* soldier was looking out his window, looking right up here, right this very instant.

"When will he come home?" I asked my mother.

"The minute this war is over."

"But when? When will it be over?"

She rubbed my fingers. One by one.

Across the terrace, a sailor and a fat lady peered through silver binoculars. A whoosh of wind puffed her dress, pumping it up and up . . . and there it was for all the world to see . . . the fat lady's *girdle*! My mother howled laughing, and so did I, and we left that place in some kind of hurry.

"I am starved, Mama."

"Any ideas?" She was teasing.

"Well"—I pretended to think it over—"well, there's always, for example, The Automat?"

"Katie! I thought you'd never ask!"

Now there was no place, anyplace, like The Automat on 42nd Street. My father called it the most fun eating establishment in all of New York City. He was right about that! The Automat was magic.

Glass-covered cubicles lined one wall. Rows and rows of them with tiny sliding doors. Behind each door was something delicious. There were hot dishes and cold, soups and drinks. But those desserts, well, they were really something! (Lemon meringue pie was my absolute very favorite.)

I paced. Back and forth. Forth and back. Sizing

up the possibilities. In the end I always chose the same thing, anyway. Egg salad on rye. A glass of milk. And, of course, lemon meringue pie.

Coins tinkled as I pushed them through each slot. I held my breath, opened a door, and— *voila!*—egg salad sandwich! More coins, another door—pie! One more nickel and one last door— milk!

We ate at a table near the window. I felt like a grown-up lady.

"I am going to write Daddy a letter," I announced, "as soon as we get home."

"Me, too." My mother sipped black coffee. "I will write him every single day, until this war is over."

"I am going to tell about that lady and her girdle," I decided. "And I will even draw a picture."

TWO

Days passed and weeks became months. My mother worked long hours in the hospital, and I went to school like always, reading away my afternoons in the public library on 100th Street. The Children's Room was upstairs on two. Wide beams of sunlight fell across dark wood tables, and the place smelled deliciously of old books.

Sometimes Miss Seacord, the librarian, said I could help. I put books on shelves and cards in files. I stamped due dates with her yellow stamper. And once in a great while, I got to read a story to the smallest children.

I loved how they crowded all around me on the Reading Rug. (It was braided and round. Raggedy, too.) They sucked at their fingers, twirled strands of hair. But they listened, really listened, to every word I said. When it was over, the littlest boy, Charley, sometimes kissed my knee.

There were just the two of us in the evening. I did my homework at the dining room table; my mother did her knitting. She was always knitting something for the soldiers. To keep their spirits warm, and their toes.

Summer arrived, then my favorite time, autumn. I turned eight in November, and winter that year came early.

I drew pictures and we sent packets of mail to my father, and he sent long letters back. They were chatty and they sounded the way *he* sounded. He told about loving our letters and about hanging my pictures near his cot. I wondered if that cot had a puffy quilt, like the warm one I used on cold, windy nights.

My mother read the letters aloud, then alone, and often she read them aloud again. Sometimes, in the middle of the night, I could hear her muffled crying. She was missing my father and I hated that most, her crying.

We went to the temple on Friday nights. The rabbi talked and talked, but I didn't mind. I liked the way his voice sounded. He spoke of war and brave soldiers and of better days coming. He asked us all to help in some small way. I wondered how I could do that. The rabbi talked on, and I snuggled up close to my mother.

We walked home slowly on darkened streets. "I hate the war," I told my mother.

"I hate it, too."

"I wish Daddy were here with us now, walking too fast and singing off-key."

"I wish it, too."

"Does he remember my face?" I worried.

"Your face?"

"This face, Mama, with freckles and this nose that looks like a baby nose."

"He remembers that face." She was sure.

"But, Mama"—more worries—"what if he comes home from war and it's late at night when the lights are out, and he forgets his key and we are sound asleep and . . . ?"

"He will ring the buzzer the way he always does when he forgets that key, Katie. You and I, we'll get right up and open the door and hug him so hard he'll beg for mercy!"

"And we'll make midnight tea."

"Your father loves his tea."

I smiled in the night, tugging a bit at my coat sleeves. Those sleeves were awfully short—or maybe my arms just stretched—but there wasn't money, not this year, for a new wool coat.

Anyway, it was nearly March again. Winter would soon be over.

Louise came to us on a blowy night.

She came in a cape of royal blue velvet. It had a hood. Underneath, her hair was cut in short black layers. When she shook it, laughing, snowflakes flew everywhere.

My mother unlatched the front door and they fell into each other's arms, two best friends. Long ago they grew up together, right here in this neighborhood. They lived in the same apartment building and went to the same schools, shared clothes and books and once, they said, they even shared a boyfriend! But Louise had moved to Massachusetts and married, and now her husband was a soldier, too.

We hung her cape above the bath to dry. We put up the kettle and sliced thick chunks of bread to spread with jam. Mama brought out white-lace napkins. This was an occasion!

Now, Louise's eyes were big and blue. But her stomach, that was just plain *big*! She was going to have a baby. In a month or so.

"Imagine *me* with a baby!" she said to my mother.

"I can't imagine that!" Mama was teasing.

Then Louise's face got all cloudy. "Me with a baby . . . and Jack over there. . . ." Her eyes filled up and tears spilled out.

"But Jack may soon be home. . . . This war will end . . . sometime." My mother tried to comfort her.

Louise cried on. Then my mother started in, and I did, too.

Our tea cooled; the bread went untouched.

Suddenly my mother brightened. "Of course!" She waved her arms with excitement. "You must— of course—you must stay here, with us!"

"Stay here?" Louise sniffed.

"You can't be alone at a time like this. Not with a baby on the way. We'll take care of you, won't we, Katie? And we'll see that you take care of yourself— you look dreadful, by the way, you need to rest, Louise—and you'll deliver your baby right here in the city. I will be there with you, I promise. . . ."

"But you have your Katie to care for, and your work at the hospital—"

"No buts." Mama meant business. "You are staying with us, Louise. In fact, you must move into Katie's room. It's a fine big room that faces the river. Katie will sleep on the living room couch—"

"Mama, no!" I yelled. "That's not fair!"

She gave me a look, but I was mad.

Louise stood up. She walked all through the living room and the dining room, then she came back to the kitchen.

"I've thought it over," she said. "I will accept your generous offer. But! There are two conditions."

Mama frowned.

"Number one," said Louise. "I sleep on the living room sofa. Number two," she continued, "I am not treated like a guest in this house. I do everything you do. I help with the cooking and cleaning and—"

"No! No! No!" said my mother.

"Then back I go, to Massachusetts."

Two best friends glared at each other across the table. I wondered what would happen. I didn't have to wonder too long, though, because they just burst out laughing.

It was settled. Just like that.

Louise would stay. On the living room couch.

She unzipped her plaid valise and handed me a small red box.

There were chocolates inside. My favorites, with caramel centers.

Now there were three of us in the evening. Louise and my mother did their knitting and their talking. They told stories by the hour!

"Do you remember the time we skipped school, Louise?"

"*You* skipped school?" I stared at my mother.

The best friends giggled, remembering a concert at Radio City Music Hall, a singer with blue eyes.

"And what about those Saturday afternoons at the movies?"

"We drove your brother absolutely crazy!" Mama shook her head. "You and I, Louise, we smelled like pickles and popcorn. Sam wouldn't sit in the row with us. Bigshot Sam with his bigshot friends!"

The President spoke on the radio and the war raged on.

Louise taped a map to the dining room wall. She pointed to a pink patch in Europe.

"My Jack is somewhere near here," she told me in a brave voice.

"My father is around here, I think." I traced a path with my finger, across and down, to a place called Australia. "Did you know, Louise, over there it's still summer . . . and here in New York, we're freezing!"

Louise patted her stomach. Then she sat down to write a letter.

Sometimes she picked me up at the library. She liked to look around the Children's Room.

"I came here, too, when I was a girl," she whispered.

"Did you read a lot?"

"My brother, Sam, he was the reader." Louise laughed. "Mostly I made lists. Books to Read. Teachers I Like. Chores I Hate."

She held the banister on the way down, stopping to rest every third or fourth step.

"I wish this baby would hurry up," she joked. "A person gets tired of waiting."

"Do you think it's a boy baby or a girl?" I asked.

"Well, I used to think girl. Definitely girl. Then I changed my mind. This one's a *kicker*—must be a boy. But just recently, I changed my mind again. . . ."

We walked up Riverside Drive. The sun, big and orange, was hanging low, an inch, it seemed, from the Hudson River.

"What will you call it?" I asked Louise.

"Jack and I make lists of names." She smiled. "Our letters are all filled up with them."

"But which are your favorites?"

"My boy list is narrowed down to this: Peter, Hank, Harry, Tom, and Jed. And if it's a girl: Roya, Denise, Claire, and Deirdre."

"That's a lot of names, still, to choose from."

"Do you like *any*?" she asked.

I did not answer.

"Surely there's one?"

"There is one"—I was thinking it over—"but it isn't on your list, Louise."

"Go ahead, tell me."

"Well," I said, "the name I like is Rosie."

"Rosie?" Louise nodded. Then she smiled. "I will put it on my list."

"Put it way at the top." I laughed out loud. "Rosie! Rosie! Rosie!"

THREE

It was holiday time. The apartment hummed
with tradition. My mother brought down her good
china and the white-lace tablecloth that had been
her mother's once. It was faded in spots but very
beautiful. My mother loved that tablecloth. She
stroked it with her fingers and held it to her cheek.
She ironed out every wrinkle, then draped it over
the dining table. Louise polished silver candlesticks
and she cooked like crazy. There were last-minute
trips to the butcher, and I ran to the flower shop for
lilacs.

23

Mrs. Leitstein brought a jar of soup. "Happy Passover," she said.

"You look pretty," I whispered.

"I know that." She winked. Her dress was pink, her beads long and pearly.

We lit two candles and said Hebrew prayers. There were small glasses with wine for the grown-ups, and grape juice for me. We ate and we sang and I asked the Four Questions. It was a good time, almost. But I kept on thinking about my father and wishing he were here. Probably my mother was wishing it, too.

Someone else came, though, right around dessert time. Another soldier, home on leave. Louise's brother, Sam. Louise ran into his arms before he was in the door, even.

We served him soup, and pot roast with gravy, sweet potatoes, and apples. Then he had seconds. This Sam was hungry! He ate and he talked. About the war and family, about the war and friends, and things you don't know to miss until you haven't got them.

Afterward, he took Mrs. Leitstein home to her apartment. She leaned on his arm and they walked, slowly, down the marble steps.

April came, and the very next day, a surprise blizzard! It began before noon, and by three, when I left school, the blanket of snow reached halfway to my knees. This was really something. Happily, I headed for the library.

"You better go home," warned Miss Seacord. "Looks like a big one."

"I love it, don't you?"

"Yes, I do. But choose your books quickly, Katie, and do not dawdle. Your mother will worry."

Louise was posted on the stoop of our building. Her velvet cape blew out behind her.

"I was just coming to look for you!" she called through the snow. "Where have you been!"

We went upstairs and she rubbed my feet with a towel. I drank hot chocolate, munching away on sugar cookies.

Wind howled at the kitchen window, and rattled it, too.

"I wish Mama were home. She ought to be home from work by now."

"She will come soon." Louise boiled water in the kettle, and set out more cookies for my mother.

I drew a picture, then pasted it on a cardboard frame.

"This is me and this is you, Louise, and *this* is

your little baby in its brand-new carriage," I explained. "Here we are walking on Broadway, showing off your baby, which is beautiful, of course, and people are peeking under the netting and . . ."

"Ugh." Louise made a funny noise. Then she made a face.

"Don't you like my picture? Do you think the carriage should be red instead of silver, is that what you think, Louise?"

"It's not that." Louise forced a smile. "It's . . . I'm in labor."

"In what?" I said.

"Labor," she answered. "The baby is coming."

"Now?" I was horrified. "The baby is coming now, in a blizzard?"

Louise called the doctor. She spoke in a whisper.

"The doctor says it's time to go to the hospital," she reported calmly. "He says I better get there fast."

"You can't go now, Louise. It's snowing like crazy," I said. "Maybe later would be better."

"Now, Katie."

"But what about Mama? She is supposed to go there with you . . . she said so herself. . . ."

"I don't think there's time." Louise was chewing her lip.

"But you can't go alone! Who will take you?"

Louise grinned.

I knew right then who would take her to the hospital.

Me.

And I was scared.

We left a note on the table for my mother:

> Baby time. We've gone to the hospital.
> Love, Katie & Louise

I pulled on my boots and my coat, and my father's favorite muffler. And I charged down the stairs.

"You'll fall," scolded Mrs. Cook from her landing. "Careful, Katie!"

Hail a cab, Louise had told me.

I looked up and down the street. No taxi. I ran to Riverside Drive as best I could. Clumps of snow dropped down my boots. Oh, cold! No taxis, though. Not even one. Or buses, either. And the only cars were parked cars, half hidden in the deep, deep drifts.

Hail a cab, Louise had told me. I couldn't let her down.

Snow was sticking to my face and my lashes and I could barely see the streetlights. *Hail a cab . . . hail a cab.*

But there were none on Broadway, either.

Louise waited on the stoop. Her cape was nearly white now, with flecks of blue coming through.

"Nothing doing?" she called. "Not one little taxi?"

I shook my head.

Louise shuddered and I was scared.

"How many blocks to the hospital?" I asked.

"Four or five and they are long blocks, Katie."

Now *I* shuddered. Where was Mama?

"This baby is coming." Louise spoke very, very slowly. "Soon, I think. . . ."

"We will walk." I said it in a strange, strong voice.

"I can't. . . ."

"We will walk." I said it again, and I took her arm and led her down three steps to the snow-covered sidewalk. "I will help you and we will walk and you will get to the hospital and then you will have the baby."

"I just can't. . . ."

"You cannot have the baby out here in a blizzard, Louise."

So we walked. And trudged. And plodded. We stopped often; Louise needed to rest. I squeezed her hand and we walked. We trudged and plodded and stopped, and four blocks were never longer. My feet felt like lead feet and snow blew all around us in great, cold swirls. On and on.

"You know, this baby is going to be a special baby." I talked a lot. "It will be a snow baby. We'll call it Snow if you can't think up another name. Do you like that name, Snow, do you like it, Louise?"

The sign said WOMEN'S HOSPITAL.

"Help us!" I yelled. "We're going to have a baby!"

Silhouette-people flew down hospital steps. They scooped up Louise in her royal blue cape and she was gone. A lady with pink cheeks showed me to the waiting room.

A man was there, reading magazines and tapping his foot.

He didn't talk, though.

I waited and waited. My fingers were frozen, and my toes. And I wanted my mother.

A nurse came by. "Are you Katie?" she asked. Her face was friendly.

"Mmm-hmm."

"I have a message," said the nurse. "From Louise."

"A message?"

"It's a girl." The nurse smiled. "Louise says to tell you her name is Rosie."

My mother came. I ran into her arms and I cried.

FOUR

ROSIE WAS TINIER than anything, and she smelled like dusting powder. I loved everything about her, and Louise said I could hold her whenever I wanted.

One day, when they were out walking, I moved Rosie's pink cradle and all her nighties and sweater sets and piles of cloth diapers into my room. I put Louise's plaid valise in a corner. And I made a sign—ROSIE'S ROOM (LOUISE'S TOO). I decorated my sign with a picture. It was a picture of a little girl and her mother.

Louise hugged me and she kissed my cheek.

My mother smiled and I felt good, and I wished I'd done it sooner.

After school I took Rosie for long walks in her carriage. I changed her clothes often, and even her diaper. I showed her books and pictures and told her all about third grade and the library and how she was born in an April blizzard. I told her the war would soon be over. Then, I promised, she would meet her daddy.

The months slipped by, and I turned nine.

When Rosie was one, we had a party. Mrs. Leitstein baked a cake. We sang and Rosie clapped. Then she said her first word, and it sounded to me like "Katie."

Then came the bad day. The worst day ever.

It was hot and we were on our way to Coney Island for an afternoon at the sea—Louise and Rosie, Mama and me. There would be rides and hot dogs at Nathan's. And of course cotton candy, my favorite kind that looked like rainbows. "We are going . . . we are going . . . to fabulous, wonderful Coney Island!" I sang boldly, and skipped down the stairs.

But someone was walking up the stairs. A stranger in a uniform and black leggings. Telegram man.

"Hello, little girl." I wished he'd go away. He took off his cap and pulled an envelope from his pouch, an envelope with stars on it. "I am looking for a Mrs. . . ."

I knew right that second—and Mama, clutching the banister, she knew it, too—the news was bad. It couldn't be worse.

My father had died over there.

My father had died in the war.

We lit a candle and neighbors came. They brought cookies and cakes and everyone whispered. I wished they would leave. All I wanted was to hug my mother.

I sat on the couch and Rosie crawled onto my lap. I played with her fingers, maybe. Or maybe I didn't. So she cried . . . but that might have been me.

The days blurred together and weeks passed somehow.

Mama tied my father's letters with ribbons and she read them one by one. Then she started again at the beginning. We snuggled on her bed, or the sofa, looking at old family photos. We did that by the hour.

"Now, this is me," explained my mother. "Here I am, of course I'm younger, but you can tell it's me and I am in a park upstate and your father has fixed this fabulous picnic. . . ."

"Daddy, cook?" I asked.

And she smiled in a funny way and bragged he knew a thing or two about making a picnic.

"Show me the picture of me when I was a baby." I asked for that one again and again. There I was, all wrapped in a blanket, and my father was holding me. I wore the silliest hat, but his was sillier, even. That picture made me laugh.

Autumn came and I went back to school, and to the library afterward. Secretly, I looked for a letter from my father. There were no more letters, though. And in the night, I heard my mother's muffled crying. Night after night. And I cried, too.

But there was always Rosie. By now she was putting words together to make a sentence. Her hair grew long enough to need a bright ribbon. She learned to walk instead of waddle, and she learned to run and climb.

"Katie read a book! Katie read now!" She was bossier than anything, but I didn't mind.

"This is a bear." I sat with her on the faded

couch, cozy as ever and reading. "Now, where is his sweater? I will give you a hint; it's a blue sweater, Rosie. Like the sky."

"Love Katie!" Sometimes she stroked my hair and my face with her fat little fingers and I felt good all over. Sometimes I forgot she wasn't all mine, like a sister.

"Let me see that gorgeous little girl," Mrs. Leitstein called from the landing one afternoon.

So I brought Rosie to her, and she rubbed her crinkled cheek against Rosie's smooth one. And Mrs. Leitstein closed her eyes, softly humming, lost somehow in another time. I wondered if she were lonely.

Rosie threw her head back, laughing.

"I am very good with little children." Mrs. Leitstein winked. "So are you, I see."

"Thank you," I said, glad she had noticed. And I wanted to ask, *Are you lonely, Mrs. Leitstein?*

"Come, Katie. I am cooking soup." She waved a finger at me. "It is time you learned about chicken soup."

I took Rosie upstairs to Louise. Then I stood at Mrs. Leitstein's stove, watching every little thing she did.

"Big pot, Mrs. Leitstein."

"Fifty years, I've cooked my soup right here." She tapped the old-time pot with two knuckles. "In the best of times, and in bad times, too."

"What are those?"

"Greens and barley, onions, and of course, the chicken."

She showed me how to slice carrots. I cut up two and ate some slivers. I kneeled on a step stool, sprinkling salt and pepper over the pot like some cooking magician. This was fun! Not too much salt, warned Mrs. Leitstein. Not too little, either. I got up then and did a dance right on that stool—the Chicken Soup Cha-Cha—and we giggled.

Mrs. Leitstein stirred with a long wooden spoon and I used a little one, for tasting.

"Please," I said, "please come tonight for dinner. We will light the Sabbath candles."

Mrs. Leitstein shook her head. "Your mother has no time for guests. What with her work in the hospital, and you, Louise, and Rosie . . . Your mama has her own troubles. . . . She doesn't need me, too."

"But we do!" I said. "Besides, Mrs. Leitstein, you're no guest. You are just like family."

"Just like family . . . I like the way that sounds."

Mrs. Leitstein kissed my cheek in the gentlest way. "Thank you," she whispered, and I felt good all over.

I flew out the door, then came back.

"We eat at seven on Fridays, Mrs. Leitstein, and I will set the table. I always do on Fridays"—I winked the way she did—"I make it very pretty."

"Well then, I will bring soup," she called up the stairs. "Won't *they* be surprised when we tell them who made it!"

FIVE

WHEN MY ROSIE was two years old, her father wrote the best letter ever. He was coming home.

Soldiers came back—lots of them—but not my father.

Rosie's father hugged Louise and he scooped up the little girl he didn't yet know. They went out walking—the three of them, a family. He was nice, Rosie's father, but he was taking them home to Massachusetts.

They left us on a breezy day.

Louise squeezed me until I thought all the air would be squeezed right out of me. "I love you like a daughter," she said. And then, "I will never forget our blizzard, Katie. . . ."

". . . and the walk to the hospital," I added.

"Was it a million miles?"

"Only four blocks."

"But we made it, didn't we." Louise smiled at Rosie, high on her father's shoulders. And I thought about my father, who had strong shoulders, too.

Louise cried when she hugged my mother and my mother cried, too, and they drove away in their little car. It was green.

Mama and I went upstairs but it was too, too quiet.

So we went down again and we walked in the park, arm in arm, buttoning our sweaters against the wind. Afterward, Mrs. Leitstein gave us soup. She served it piping hot with noodles.

A few weeks later, on a stormy night, we had a surprise visitor. It was Sam again, Louise's brother.

"Why, Sam!" my mother cried. "Come in out of the rain. . . . You'll catch a nasty cold. . . ."

"Louise told me the news. . . . I'm so sorry. . . ." He talked about my father while I hung his yellow slicker above the bath to dry.

My mother made coffee. There were warm biscuits, too. And strawberry preserves from the porcelain jar that Sam brought.

"I feel like I'm dreaming, the best of dreams, too . . . home again . . . back in the States." He looked around our little apartment like he was looking at a castle. "How old are you now, Katie?"

"Ten," I said.

"Ten already!" Sam whistled. "You are tall."

"I am tall," I boasted, "just like my father."

"I always hoped that I would grow a few more inches." Sam shrugged. "I guess it's too late now."

"What will you do now that the war is over?" asked my mother. "Have you found a place?"

Sam shook his head. "I'm not sure, yet, about anything."

I went to my room to read a story—or maybe I would write one down—but Sam and my mother kept on talking. Mostly about the old days, I think.

He left in the rain. It was nearly midnight.

My mother kept on at the hospital.

I wrote long letters to Louise in Massachusetts, and little short ones to Rosie. Once a week I got mail back.

"Mama! Rosie got a haircut!"

"Mama! Rosie caught a butterfly!"

"Mama! They are coming to visit!"

My mother was writing, too. She wrote to Louise and to Rosie and to someone else, besides. Sam, Louise's brother. Now he was living in a faraway state called Texas.

Sam wrote fat letters and Mama read them out loud in the evening. He sounded like a good time, I thought, although I never said it.

"Funny thing for a city boy," said my mother, "to build himself a ranch."

"How come he did it?"

"A new start." She was thoughtful. "Sam wanted a brand-new start."

"But Texas? It's so far away! It's hot there, and dusty." I clicked my tongue. "He must be lonely, Mama."

"Mmm-hmm."

"Unless . . . well . . . maybe he met a lady—a ranchy sort of lady—maybe he'll get married!"

"No!" My mother looked surprised. "Not Sam."

"You think Sam Gold is handsome"—I paused—"like Daddy?"

"No," she said, "not like Daddy. But Sam is sweet, really sweet, don't you think so, Katie?"

"I don't know . . . maybe," I said, and I went inside to eat a chocolate.

Then Sam wrote a letter just to me. That was fun, getting a letter from Texas, but I wondered why he wrote it.

Dear Katie,

How are you? I hope you are enjoying school.

Your mother says you draw beautiful pictures. I draw, too, but mine are mostly scribbles. Maybe sometime you'll send me a picture, if you have a chance.

This ranch is big and it is getting greener every month. A little quiet for a city sort of fellow. Beautiful, though, and there is peace.

My cow, Elvira, is about to have babies!
Sincerely yours,
Sam Gold

I stuffed his letter in a drawer.
"Maybe you'll write back?" suggested my mother.
"I don't think so," I said.
She went inside to roast a chicken.
I followed in a minute and started scraping carrots. I washed potatoes at the sink and patted them dry with a towel. "Why did Sam write me a letter?" I asked my mother.

"He likes you, I guess."

"How can he like me?" I said. "He doesn't even *know* me!"

"Maybe he wants to, Katie." She smiled. "You're not so bad to know."

"Well," I told her, "I do not like writing letters."

My mother didn't answer. She knew it was a lie.

But Sam was persistent. He wrote to me again. And then again. He told about the books he read and the color of his couch. He told about surprise frosty mornings and about life on a ranch. His letters were fun, and he scribbled pencil drawings in the corners. *This is a picture of me, big city fellow, holding a rake!* Or, *Here are Elvira's chubby calves . . . arrived Friday 4* A.M. *. . . anyway, they are cute!*

I shared each letter with my mother. She laughed at Sam's drawings. I liked that, when she laughed.

"Have you written yet to Sam?" she asked from time to time.

"No, Mama. Not yet."

"It's plain rude, Katie, not to write back."

I knew it was rude but I wasn't ready. Not yet.

"But why?" she said in a soft, sad voice. "Why not just give Sam a chance?"

"Later, maybe."

I went downstairs to visit Mrs. Leitstein. She was all dressed up and she wore a lacy shawl.

"Today is my anniversary," she explained.

"But . . ."

"Dear Mr. Leitstein, gone so many years. I loved him," she whispered, "in the good times and the hard times, too. I love him still." Mrs. Leitstein's eyes were bright. She pointed to a photograph on the mantel, and took it down to show me.

"He was very handsome," I said, admiring the picture.

"You bet your whiskers!" Mrs. Leitstein straightened. We were just about the same size now.

I sucked in my breath. "I have a problem," I said.

Mrs. Leitstein took my hand and she took me to the kitchen. It smelled wonderfully of warm pound cake. She cut a fat slice for me, and for herself, a sliver. There was milk, too, in a bright yellow pitcher.

"Well then, Katie, tell me about your problem."

I blurted it out. The words kept coming. "It's just that Sam Gold—you know, Louise's brother—he writes to Mama all the time from Texas!" I began.

"Go on."

"And she writes back!"

"Go on."

"And now I get letters, too, and Mama says I'm rude because I don't write back. It's not that he isn't nice. Sam *is* nice, Mrs. Leitstein, and I plan to write him maybe, sometime. Mama says give him a chance, but why should I! What should I do!"

"You miss your father." Her words filled the room.

And there I was, swallowing back tears, or maybe I wasn't, because there she was, wiping them off my cheeks. I dropped across her lap and Mrs. Leitstein stroked my hair and I cried, and the crying felt good.

"Love is risky," she said after a while, "but you know something, Katie?"

"What?" I asked.

"It's worth it." She kissed the picture of Mr. Leitstein. Then she kissed my forehead.

And she sent me home for dinner.

That night I drew a picture of a man on a ranch. He wore black boots. There were horses, too, and a girl (she was tallish) way in the corner near the barn. That girl was wearing blue jeans and they were new and stiff, and she was wearing old party shoes that looked like city shoes. But she didn't care because there she was, checking up on some new-born calves.

I put the picture in an envelope and I sent it all the way to Texas. I hoped Sam Gold would like it.

Then one day, many months later, a skinny letter came, one that made my mother twirl through the rooms like a dancer.

"Sam wants us to come to Texas!"

"What for?" I said, and "Why?"

"A brand-new start." She hugged me until my feet were off the ground. "A brand-new start in Texas!"

We packed and packed. The rooms were rented to a lady and her daughter, and neighbors came to say good-bye. Mrs. Leitstein wept. I promised to send her a picture a week. Lots of letters, too. Mrs. Leitstein was family.

There were no soldiers at Pennsylvania Station, or women waving hankies. But an ancient man was selling chestnuts from a crooked wooden wagon.

This train had sleeping berths and a whole entire car just for dining. The tables were all set up with bleached-white cloths and silver sugar bowls and plates that looked like Mama's good china.

We rode and rode.

Outside there were trees and grass, and clusters of houses. I kept my nose pressed to the window and warm tears—silent tears—dripped down my collar. I kept a book on my lap and blank paper beside me. South and west. We rode and rode.

I asked the same questions over and over.

"When is the wedding, Mama?"

"A week from next Thursday."

"Will you wear a white dress?"

"Navy blue, and it will be a suit."

"What if Sam doesn't like me?"

"He likes you already." Mama was sure.

"I might just *hate* that ranch and Texas."

"It will take getting used to."

"And what about Daddy?" There. I said it.

"You and I will love him always. Forever," she added, and she rubbed my fingers. One by one.

"Love is risky," I told her then, "but you know something, Mama?"

"What?" she asked.

"It's worth it."

And she smiled because she already knew that, I think.

Dust blew in the windows and it was hot. We passed through brown deserts and little towns with buildings that looked like shacks. And sometimes there were green fields that stretched on for hours. At night, from my berth, I watched the bright stars. And in the morning we dined like fancy ladies. We rode west and we rode south.

A boy in patched overalls pushed a wheelbarrow. He looked nice, and the train stopped and we were in Texas.

Sam wore a suit and he brought two flowers.
One for my mother.
The other one for me.
Then we went home to get ready for a wedding.